hc

The Usborne
Little Book
of
Trees

First published in 2008 by Usborne Publishing Ltd.,
Usborne House, 83-85 Saffron Hill, London, EC1N 8RT, England
www.usborne.com

Printed in Dubai

The Usborne Little Book of Trees

Phillip Clarke

Designed by Michael Hill,
Marc Maynard and Kate Rimmer

Digital manipulation by Keith Furnival

Consultant: Derek Patch
Director of the Tree Advice Trust

Edited by Kirsteen Rogers

Internet links

There are lots of fun websites where you can find out more about trees. We have created links to some of the best sites on the Usborne Quicklinks Website. To visit the sites, go to www.usborne-quicklinks.com and type in the keywords "little trees". Here are some of the things you can do on the internet:

🍁 Learn to spot leaves by playing sudoku
🍁 Help a tree to make an album of its memories
🍁 Start an online nature diary, to record the trees you see

Tree pictures to download

You can download many of the pictures in this book from the Usborne Quicklinks Website. These pictures are for personal use only and must not be used for commercial purposes.

Internet safety

The websites recommended in Usborne Quicklinks are regularly reviewed. However, the content of a website may change at any time and Usborne Publishing is not responsible for the content of websites other than its own. We recommend that children are supervised while on the internet.

Respecting nature

When visiting woods and forests, always remember to follow this code:

• Never light fires • Keep to the paths, and close gates behind you
• Keep dogs under control • Don't damage hedges, fences, walls or signs
• Look, don't touch: leave plants, animals and nests alone • Leave no litter

Contents

6 What is a tree?

8 Types of tree

10 Lush leaves

12 Root and branch

14 Sturdy trunks

16 A tree is born

18 Taking shape

20 Spring blooms

22 Fruit and seeds

26 Autumn glory

28 Trees in winter

30 Growing old

32 Death and afterlife

34 Wild woods

38 Hangers-on

40 Pine woods

42 Oak woods

44 Beech woods

46 Wet woods

48 Town trees

50 Wood is good

52 Forest harvest

54 Working with trees

56 Protecting trees

58 Trees of the world

60 Tree tales

62 Amazing but true

64 Index

What is a tree?

Trees are the Earth's ancient giants. They can grow bigger than any other plant and live longer than any animal.

High and mighty

Most trees have one trunk, a thick stem that rises some way above the ground before branching into twiggy boughs. Fully grown, trees are usually at least 6m (20ft) tall, and many grow several times higher.

With its sturdy wooden trunk, this Douglas fir tree may grow to 60m (200ft).

Scots pines like these were overlooking this valley before the first people settled there.

Tree or shrub?

Woody plants under 6m (20ft), with several stems, are known as shrubs. Some plants that are trees in the wild can be shrubs if kept trimmed.

A clipped Leyland cypress makes a neat bush uncut, it can grow into a 40m (130ft) monster.

Long lives

For many plants, life is over in a few short months, but a tree's stiff trunk and tough bark let it survive year after year. Some trees live for many centuries.

Giant sequoias can live for over 3,000 years.

The older a tree, the greater the range of living things it supports.

Protecting life

Trees provide shelter for thousands of animal and plant species, and their leaves, fruits and seeds are food for many more. Their roots hold soil in place, while their leaves make oxygen gas that people and animals need to breathe. Without trees, little could survive.

Fieldfares feast on rowan berries.

Treecreepers spiral up tree trunks, hunting for insects.

Nut weevils lay their eggs in acorns.

Toadstools often appear at the foot of trees.

Butterflies feed on fallen fruit.

Types of tree

There are over 80,000 kinds of tree in the world. Whether they grow in well-kept parks or tangled forests, most of them belong to one of two groups: conifers and broadleaves.

Needles and scales

Conifers have tough little leaves shaped like needles or scales. They are usually evergreen, which means they stay on the tree all year, only falling off when new leaves grow. Most young conifers are rocket-shaped, with straight trunks.

Shore pine needles

Giant sequoia scales

Sitka spruces grow very tall and straight.

Cone bearers

Conifers were named because their seeds grow in woody cones (the word "conifer" means "cone-bearer"). The seeds lie tucked safely in between the scales of the cones until they're ripe and ready to be released.

This Scots pine cone has opened to allow its ripe seeds to scatter.

Douglas fir cone

Broadleaf trees

Broadleaves have bigger, wider leaves than conifers, with more varied shapes. Many trees are deciduous, losing their leaves each autumn. Their trunks often divide into several main branches, making them bushier than conifers. Broadleaves bear a wide variety of fruits, ranging from rosy apples to wizened walnuts.

Sweet chestnut seeds are cased inside prickly fruits.

London plane leaves have ragged edges. Their fruits are round and bristly.

Elder trees bear bunches of purplish-black berries.

Broadleaves are often not as symmetrical as conifer trees.

Sweet chestnut

Common pear

Bobble fruit

Palm trees

Palm trees grow mainly in hot and steamy parts of the world known as the tropics. They're not related to conifers or broadleaves, but to lilies and grasses, and grow very differently from other trees.

Some palm leaves fan out like giant hands.

Palm trunks get taller but not wider each year, and most have no branches.

9

Lush leaves

A tree's leaves act like solar panels, soaking up energy from the Sun. They're also food factories, producing the nourishment trees need to grow.

Green power

Leaves get their green colour from a chemical called chlorophyll. This uses sunlight energy to join carbon dioxide gas from the air with water from the soil. The result is a sugary sap which trees use as food.

Some leaves also contain dark-coloured chemicals that hide chlorophyll, so the leaves don't look green, even in spring.

Copper beech

Golden holly

A few leaf types are only green in patches. They can't make as much food so they grow more slowly.

Spread out like this, these lime leaves can absorb as much light as possible.

In the pipeline

Look closely at a leaf, and you'll see a network of fine veins. These pipe watery sap up from the roots, and send sugary sap from the leaves around the tree.

Leaf shapes

Leaves come in many shapes and sizes, whether oval or pointed, long and skinny or broad and raggedy. Even on a single tree, no two leaves are exactly alike.

Lobed leaves, like this white poplar, have wiggly outlines.

A leaf from lower down on the same tree has smaller lobes.

Whitebeam leaves have jagged edges.

The leaves of white willow trees are long and slender.

Compound leaves, like this ash, are made up of several smaller leaves, called leaflets.

Each horse chestnut leaf has leaflets that splay out from a central point.

Heart-shaped lime leaves have long "drip-tips" so water can run off easily.

Conifer leaves

From a distance, conifer trees may look similar, but a closer look will soon show you that their needles and scales grow in very different ways.

Cedar needles grow mainly in rosettes.

Cypresses have tiny scales.

Pine needles grow in bunches.

Fir needles grow all along the twig.

Root and branch

A tree's branches spread widely
as it reaches for sunlight. Below the ground,
hidden from view, its roots often spread wider still.

Putting down roots

Roots anchor a tree firmly in the earth,
keeping it upright on windy days. Even
more importantly, they grow down into
the soil, soaking up water and minerals.
Roots also store a tree's winter food.

Most of a tree's
roots spread out
sideways, keeping
the trunk stable.

Piping up

Apart from lifting the leaves nearer
to energizing sunlight, the trunk's
main role is to act as a water pipe.
It channels watery sap, filled with
health-giving minerals, from the
roots up into the leaves.

Thick tree roots divide
into ever finer ones.

Thirsty work

Leaves take in air through minute
holes in their undersides. As this
happens, the leaves are dried out
by sun and wind. To replace the
moisture, a constant supply
of watery sap is drawn
up from the roots.

Air holes
(25x life
size)

Underside

The root tips are covered
in microscopic hairs which
soak up water from the soil.

A root may have to
grow around stones
or other obstacles.

Branching out

Unlike animals, trees don't stretch out as they grow, but only lengthen from the tips of their branches. Unless it breaks off, a side branch will always be the same height from the ground, no matter how thick it becomes.

A young tree's side branches begin to grow.

As the trunk grows wider and taller, the branches grow thicker and longer.

Twiggy branches once grew low on this trunk. As the tree grew, the branches withered in its shade, or were eaten by passing animals.

Pine branches

The branches of many pine trees grow in evenly spaced whorls that you may see on its trunk. A new set of branches grows each year, so counting the whorls can give you a good idea of how old a tree is.

The number of branch whorls, and scars left by branches, on the trunk of this Corsican pine shows it's about eight years old.

13

Sturdy trunks

Compared with rustling leaves or swaying branches, a tree trunk may not attract a second glance. But there's more to these woody pillars than meets the eye.

Dead and alive

Every year, a trunk gets fatter as new wood grows behind the bark. This sapwood is full of tiny tubes that carry watery sap from the roots to the leaves. As the years pass, the older tubes harden and die, forming a supportive core of heartwood.

— Bark

— Heartwood

— Sapwood

If a tree makes more food than it needs, the extra is stored in these pale rays.

Count the rings

Every tree stump tells a story. The number of rings shows how old a tree was when it was cut down. Wide rings record good growth years, with plenty of light and food. Narrow rings show years of drought or overcrowding.

By counting its rings you can see this tree was about 40 years old when it was felled.

Darker, slow-growing summer wood

Annual rings, magnified

Lighter, fast-growing spring wood

Like a trunk, branches and twigs grow in rings.

Bark

Bark is like a protective skin, keeping the living wood from drying out, being damaged, or freezing. It's made up of a waterproof outer layer on top of a corky under-bark. Tubes inside the bark carry sugary sap from the leaves around the tree.

Cork oaks grow in southern Europe. They have very thick bark, which is harvested to make bottle stoppers.

Cork

Cracking up

Bark is dead, so it can't grow or stretch. Instead, as the tree gets wider, it cracks, flakes or peels off, revealing the newer bark beneath. Some trees can be recognized just by the texture of their bark.

Beech bark crumbles off in tiny chips.

Sitka spruce bark breaks off in big flakes.

Sycamore bark falls off in large pieces.

Silver birch bark peels away in strips.

Paper birches, like this, are named because of their peeling, parchment-like bark.

A tree is born

Most trees grow from seeds. All winter, a seed lies in the cool earth. Inside it, the beginnings of a baby tree await the gentle warmth of the weak spring sunshine.

Springing up

In spring, the seed takes in water, and swells up. Its first root burrows into the soil, and a slender shoot pushes upwards. Seed leaves open to receive light, and a tender bud appears.

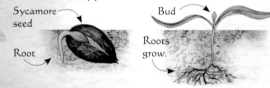

Sycamore seed

Root

Bud

Roots grow.

One day, this fragile seedling may be a mighty oak tree.

The little root grows down, reaching the water and minerals it needs.

Seed leaves are a different shape from later leaves. A bud nestles between them.

Summer seedlings

In summer, the bud opens and the true leaves of the young tree, or seedling, unfold. A new bud forms at the base of each leaf.

True leaves unfold.

No longer needed, the seed leaves wither and die.

The acorn shell rots away as the young tree grows.

Autumn and winter

When autumn comes, the leaves die and fall off, leaving scars on the stem. Throughout the winter, the "leader" bud, at the tip of the shoot, is protected by leaf-like bud scales.

Leader bud grows into a main shoot.

Side buds grow into side shoots.

Leaf scar

Inside a bud

Bud scale

Leaves tightly packed, like a Brussels sprout

Growing up

In a seedling's second spring, its buds open and the bud scales fall off, leaving scars. Through spring and summer, the buds unfurl their new leaves for that year, and the shoots grow longer. This cycle of growth will carry on throughout its life.

First summer

Leader bud

Seed leaves were here

Bud scale scar

Second summer

Suckers

Sometimes, new trees are made without seeds, by putting up new shoots from their roots. These are called suckers.

Western balsam poplar often spreads using sucker roots.

Third summer

Bud scale scar

Taking shape

Different tree types have distinctive shapes. There's often variation between individual trees, too, as they grow reacting to their surroundings.

At a glance

Some trees can be recognized just by their outlines, or the way their branches are arranged. You can see this best in winter, when many trees are leafless.

This Norway spruce's cone-like shape is typical of young conifers.

Scots pine has a bare trunk.

Ashes grow tall and very open at the top.

Weeping willow branches droop gracefully down.

Lombardy poplars are elegant trees with tightly packed, upright branches.

Living room

The shape of a developing tree is strongly influenced by the number of other trees growing nearby.

English oaks in open spaces grow into a rounded shape.

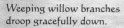

In a crowded forest, oaks grow taller and thinner as they fight for light.

Sun, rain and snow

Local climates around the world affect both the type of trees suited to growing there, and the shape of particular trees.

Western hemlock grows in the snowy mountains of North America. Its short, bendy branches slope down so that snow slides off.

This stone pine grows in Italy. Its shallow, umbrella shape lets hot, drying winds slip easily past.

Trees in hot, wet rainforests grow all year round, shooting up on skinny trunks as they compete for sunlight.

Wind sculpture

Trees growing by the coast or on hillsides are often shaped by the wind. They can take the most fantastic forms as they struggle to survive the gusts and gales.

The constant buffeting of salty sea storms has forced this juniper to grow branches on its more sheltered side.

Spring blooms

As spring arrives, tree buds burst open, unfolding their new leaves and flowers. Flowers that grow on trees, especially fruit trees, are often known as blossoms.

Flower power

Some tree flowers are big and showy; others are so small they hardly seem like flowers at all. However they look, they all have a vital job: producing seeds to make new trees.

This splendid magnolia bloom is one of the largest flowers of any tree.

Elm flowers are tiny red specks.

Elder trees have clusters of little white flowers.

Male and female

Blossoms are male or female, or have male and female parts in a single flower. To make seeds, the females must first be sprinkled with pollen, a powder made by the males. This is known as pollination.

Beech trees have both male and female flowers.

Female

Male

Male

Female

Rowan flowers have male and female parts.

On the breeze

Trees can't travel around, so they
need help to spread their pollen.
Some use the wind to carry it.
They tend to have clusters of
tiny flowers with no petals.

Larch has pink-
tipped female
flowers that grow
on its upper branches...

...Pollen drifts upwards
from yellow male flowers
on the lower branches.

Male and female
crack willow
flowers grow on
separate trees.

Like many
wind-pollinated
trees, crack willows
have fuzzy flower
clusters called catkins.

The wind
shakes out
the pollen.

Male

Female

Hired help

Some trees use insects to carry their pollen. They
attract them with fragrant-petalled flowers, and
a sweet liquid called nectar. As the bees sip the
nectar, they become coated with pollen, which
rubs off onto the next flowers they then visit.

This bee is carrying
pollen in "baskets"
on its legs.

Bees visit apple
blossom in the
afternoon, when
the nectar is
at its richest.

Bees can tell which horse
chestnut flowers are making
nectar by their yellow marks.

Fruit and seeds

If you think of fruit, the first things that spring to mind are often colour, shape and taste. But to a tree, the most important part is the seed inside.

From flowers to fruit

After a flower is pollinated, its petals drop off, and it develops into a fruit. The fruit's job is to keep its seeds safe inside until they're ripe, and then to get them far enough away from the tree to grow. This is so new trees don't have to compete with their parent for space, light and water.

Section of rowan berry, showing seeds

Pear

Rowan berries

Some fruits, such as apples, pears and rowan berries, hold their seeds in a fleshy core.

Mulberries are made up of berry-like parts, each with its own seed.

This is the remains of the flower.

Apple

Fruits such as plums and cherries have a single, hard seed.

Figs are unusual fruits: the flowers grow inside them, developing into hundreds of seeds.

Cherry

Plum

Juicy fruit

Fruit are often tasty to encourage animals to eat them and carry them away inside their bodies. The seeds later pop out in their droppings, so wherever they land, they have a little dollop of fertilizer to boost their growth.

Bullfinches eat elderberries in autumn.

Holly berries are a winter treat for woodmice.

In summer, wasps feast upon the sweet, gloopy goodness of fallen plums.

Tough nuts

Nuts are a type of dry fruit made up of a hard shell, protecting a large seed. They are packed with nourishment, and relished by animals.

Horse chestnuts, or conkers, are eaten by deer and cattle.

Walnuts have a large seed in a thin, woody shell.

If this squirrel buries its nut to eat when food is scarce but then forgets about it, the nut may sprout into a new tree.

Helicopter ride

Some trees have dry, papery fruit shaped like wings. As the wind catches them, they twirl away, carrying their seeds far and wide. Other fruits fall apart, releasing seeds with feathery parachutes that drift along on the breeze.

These maple "keys" hang on the tree until late summer, when they fall and flutter away.

Sycamore keys have two wings.

Fluffy willow catkins fall apart, releasing their seeds.

Feathery tufts keep willow seeds aloft.

Ash keys have a single wing.

Elm seeds are enclosed in papery wings.

Plane tree bobble fruits break up in the wind.

Bobble fruit seeds

Cones

On conifer trees the female flowers grow into woody cones with tough scales that protect their seeds. The scales only open to release the seeds when the weather is warm and dry.

A Scots pine cone releasing its seeds

These seeds are spread by the wind.

Birds such as this crossbill prise open cones to eat their seeds.

Norway spruce cones

Cones aren't always cone-shaped. These unripe cypress cones look more like large, dried peas.

The cones of a stone pine take three years to ripen. People harvest their edible seeds, which are known as pine nuts.

Junipers and yews have small, fleshy cones that look like berries.

Yew

Seed

Juniper

Seed

Atlas cedar cones are egg-shaped. They slowly fall apart on the branch, and their winged seeds are blown away.

Open and shut

You can see for yourself how a cone opens in dry weather, by placing a closed one near a radiator. Its scales will slowly open as it dries out.

In cold, damp weather a cone stays shut.

When the weather is warm and dry, its scales unfold.

Autumn glory

Of all seasons, autumn is often the most spectacular. As fruit ripens on their branches, many trees put on a display of fiery crimsons and oranges, golds and browns.

Goodbye to greenery

Silver maple

Winter's freezing weather is dangerous for soft, vulnerable leaves, and its short days make it hard for them to absorb sunlight. Deciduous trees prepare for this testing time by losing their leaves in autumn.

As this leaf loses its green chlorophyll and dries out, hidden colours are revealed.

The chemical that is turning these horse chestnut leaves yellow is also found in bananas.

The leaf dies and is blown off, leaving behind a scar, and a bud with next year's leaves.

All fall down

The leaves of most deciduous trees fall over a few weeks. Some, such as young beeches, keep dead leaves on their lower parts all winter, until they are replaced by new ones in spring.

Horse chestnut leaves fall as early as September.

Rowan

Trees lose their leaves at different times.

Oak leaves may drop as late as November.

A ginkgo's leaves may all fall off in one day.

Copper beech

Red oak

Make a leaf album

Autumn is the best time of year to collect fallen leaves. See how many different types you can find – a field guide will help you identify them. If you like, you could stick them into an album.

A field guide will help you to identify the leaves you find.

1. Press some clean, dry leaves between sheets of blotting paper, weighed down by heavy books.

2. Wait a few weeks, then stick the pressed leaves into a scrapbook with tape.

Trees in winter

Winter is a challenging time for many trees. While some are cloaked with leaves that can endure the cold, others stand naked to survive the season.

Wax jackets

Evergreen leaves are specially designed to withstand wintry weather. A waxy coating keeps them from freezing in the frosty air. The shape of the leaves helps them survive, too.

Long, thin Scots pine needles lose water far less easily than wider, flatter leaves.

Unlike most conifer leaves, larch needles aren't waxy, so the trees shed them in autumn.

Holly leaves are broad and flat, but their thick waterproof covering protects them.

Snowflakes can't pile up on these narrow pine needles, so even a heavy snowfall leaves only a light sprinkling

Winter buds

Without their leaves, a tree's buds and overall shapes are easier to see. A field guide will help you to identify them. Here are a few examples you could look out for:

Beech

Beech buds are brown and spiky.

Sycamore

Sycamores have large, green buds with dark-edged scales.

Sweet chestnut

Sweet chestnut has knobbly twigs and big, reddish buds.

Grow your own

If you want to watch buds open before spring, you could take a twig cutting and keep it indoors. Do ask permission from the tree's owner first.

Buds

Sturdy scissors

1. Find a tree with plump buds and snip off a few 25cm (10in) twigs. Goat willow works well.

2. Put the cuttings in a jam jar of water and leave it in a warm, sunny place indoors.

3. Keep the water topped up. In a few weeks, the buds will start to open.

Growing old

Trees may live for hundreds or thousands of years. As their trunks widen each growing season, trees can be extremely fat by the time they reach old age.

Looks can deceive

Some trees may not be the age they seem because they grow much more quickly or slowly than others. Their life span also affects when they're considered to be old.

These trees all have trunks 3m (9¾ft) around.

At 120 years, this beech is middle aged.

Cedars of Lebanon grow rapidly, for trees. This one could be just 45.

Yews grow very slowly. This one is 235, but is still in its infancy.

Signs of ageing

Apart from their size, old trees often look gnarled. Most show a history of damage, such as holes, dead branches or sap oozing out of a crack in the bark.

Ivy

Fern

Fungi such as this giant polypore often grow on old trees.

Lichen

Old trees are often festooned with ferns, lichen, ivy and other climbing plants.

Animal holes are a common sign of age in trees.

Estimating age

In open spaces, most trunks widen by about 2.5cm (1in) every year (half that in forests). This means, for example, that a lone oak whose trunk measures 2.5m (8½ft) around could be 100 years old.

Stagheads

Big, old trees sometimes outgrow the water supply their roots can provide. Their heaviest branches may then die and break off, giving them an antler-like "staghead" look.

Some old trees lose branches to save water.

Not dead yet

Trees that appear to be dead may still be surviving. Even when its heartwood has completely rotted away, a tree can still grow new leaves every year.

This oak is over 1,000 years old, and completely hollow. Amazingly, dinner parties for 20 people are said to have been held inside it.

Death and afterlife

Even a tree that lasts for a thousand years dies
eventually. But its story does not end there, as it
goes on to support the lives of many other things.

A time to die

With its tough-looking bark, a
tree may seem invincible, but even
a small injury can leave it open
to attack from fungi and insects,
leading to deadly disease. This may
finish off a tree long before its time.

Sawn branch

Trees can't
easily heal
injuries.

Three years later

They slowly
grow new bark
to seal them off.

Six years later

This takes
them a very
long time.

Scale insects
cling to bark
like limpet shells.
They infest trees,
sucking out their sap.

Scale insects

Elm bark beetles tunnel
under bark to lay their eggs.
As they do so, they spread
fungi which causes Dutch
elm disease.

Elm bark beetle

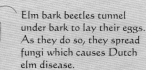

English
elm

Some fungi, such as this
dryad's saddle, invade
a tree through a wound
and grow, causing decay
that rots its heartwood.

Most of the English elms in
Britain were killed by Dutch
elm disease in the 1960s.

Dead good

A third of woodland creatures rely on dead wood for food or a place to live, so dead trees and fallen logs are vital to their survival.

Pipistrelle bat

Bats rest in tree holes during the day.

Long-eared bat

Weasels live in hollow logs or holes in dead trees.

Hollow trees make daytime hideaways for night birds such as this barn owl.

Log cabin

Creepy-crawlies are very much at home in a rotting log. Next time you pass one, look closely to see what has moved in.

Centipedes live under dead bark, scuttling out at night to hunt small insects.

Decaying wood is food for a woodlouse.

Stag beetles lay their eggs in crumbling wood in summer.

Slugs eat fungi that live on dead logs.

A stag beetle grub grows inside a rotting log for several years.

Wild woods

A wood is more than just a crowd of trees.
It's a close-knit community of living things
which depend on each other to survive.

Light and shade

From deep, dark forests where the trees
grow so tightly you can barely squeeze
through, to sunny glades and dusky
dells, woodland landscapes have very
varied levels of light. This affects which
trees and plants can grow there.

Primrose

These plants grow
in open woodland.

Multi-storey living

If a wood lets in enough light, then
shrubs will grow below its taller trees,
and, beneath them, smaller plants such
as grasses, ferns and flowers. Down on the
ground, where little light falls, mosses
and fungi make their living.

Hawthorn

Fungi often grow
on fallen wood.

Turkey
tail fungus

Bluebell

Wood
blewit

Ferns

Web of life

Just as a spider's web would fall apart if its strands weren't all joined together, so all the trees and animals in a wood need each other to survive. If even one species vanishes, many others can be affected.

1. In spring, fresh, young leaves make a tasty banquet for hungry sawfly larvae.

3. Taking flight from their treetop nests, sparrowhawks weave through the trees as they hunt great tits and other small birds.

2. Great tits live among the shrubs. They may take 300 larvae in a day, to feed their chicks.

Wriggling recyclers

In nature, nothing is wasted. Even dead leaves are recycled. Earthworms and other creepy-crawlies eat them and help to break them down into humus, a dark, rich soil ingredient that helps the trees grow.

Shrews have to eat every few hours. This one is sniffing out juicy worms.

Worms tug dead leaves down into the soil, to plug their burrows, and to eat.

Bark life

Bark is always worth a second look. You might spot all sorts of tiny creatures crawling or scuttling up and down a trunk, or hiding in the nooks and crannies of its craggy surface.

Pine weevils eat the thin bark of young conifers.

This purple emperor butterfly is sucking sugary sap from broken bark with its straw-like mouthparts.

Litter bugs

The leaf litter covering a forest floor is teeming with life. Countless creatures rely on the fallen leaves for food and shelter. The leaf piles make ideal breeding and feeding grounds for moulds and other fungi, too.

Millipedes munch fallen leaves.

These white speckles are mould, which feeds on dead leaves, helping them to rot.

You might spot these creatures lurking in leaf litter.

Snail

Centipede

Most of this leaf has rotted away, leaving a delicate skeleton of lacy veins.

Woodland detective

Next time you go for a walk in the woods, keep your eyes open for clues that wildlife has been around.

These hazelnuts have been nibbled by animals in their own special ways:

Dormouse

Grey squirrel

Wood mouse

Hazel

This pine cone's seeds were roughly plucked out by a woodpecker.

The white squiggles on this bramble leaf are tunnels made by a tiny caterpillar called a leaf miner.

You may see bare branches where voles or squirrels have gnawed off the bark, as this bank vole is doing.

Dropping hints

Droppings are a sure sign that animals have passed by. Meat-eating animals leave sausage-shaped droppings with pointed ends. The droppings of plant-eaters are usually small and round.

Field vole droppings

Fallow deer droppings stick together in summer.

Rabbit droppings

Weasel droppings

Winter dropping

Hangers-on

Many living things survive by growing on others. Most live harmlessly on their "hosts", but some, called parasites, hurt them. A few actually give help in return.

Fungi

Mushrooms and toadstools belong to a group of living things called fungi that, unlike plants, can't make their own food. Most of a fungus is unseen: a tangled mass of root-like threads that delve into wood or soil, slowly digesting the matter around them.

A fly agaric's underground threads fuse with nearby birch tree roots, passing vital minerals to the tree and taking extra food from it in return.

Honey fungus like this may grow on dead or living trees, steadily rotting their wood.

Friend or foe?

Fungi such as fly agaric help trees survive. Some bracket fungi, on the other hand, are parasites that may eventually kill them.

Beef steak bracket grows on oak, doing little harm.

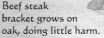

Birch bracket gradually kills the birch trees on which it lives.

A leg up

Some plants use trees for physical support, twisting and climbing around them to reach the light. Ivy does no harm, but parasites such as mistletoe can weaken a tree.

Ivy is an evergreen plant that is often seen on trees, as well as walls and houses.

Mistletoe sucks watery sap from trees, like a vampire drinking blood.

Common polypody is a fern that sometimes grows on branches.

White berries

Leafy lichen

Crusty growths

While fungi can't make food, microscopic plants called algae can. Some fungi and algae team up to form crusty growths called lichens. These often grow on old trees with ridged bark, such as oak.

Lichen only grows where the air is clean. The more leafy or branching the type of lichen, the purer the air.

Branching lichen

Bog moss (close-up)

Cushion moss

Moist moss

Moss is a simple, flowerless plant that grows best in damp places. It is often found clinging to the shadiest side of old tree trunks.

Pine woods

Pines are conifers that can grow well in places with poor soil. There are some very old, natural pine woods, but most were planted by people.

Room to grow

Most planted pine forests are dark, crowded, and littered with tough pine needles, allowing few plants to grow. But in ancient Scots pine woods that have grown naturally, there are sunny clearings where a few hardy plants can survive.

Unlike most conifers, mature Scots pines aren't cone-shaped, but often have an uneven, or flat-topped look.

Scots pines have tall trunks with reddish bark near the top.

These plants grow in old Scots pine woods.

Lower down, the bark is greyish and flaky.

Rowan berries in late summer

Twinflower

Downy birch catkins in spring

Sickener fungus breaks down pine needles, returning their goodness to the soil.

Juniper berries in autumn

Pine wildlife

Although life is hard for plants and animals in pine woods, some thrive there, and a few can only live among ancient pines.

Pine martens are rare animals related to stoats. They hunt birds and voles.

Crossbills use their overlapping beaks to tweak the seeds out of pine cones.

Long-eared owl

Wood ants gather large mounds of pine needles to protect their nests.

Red deer

Capercaillies are turkey-sized birds found only in Scottish pine woods.

Fox and cubs

Sticky stuff

Conifers, especially pines, produce a sticky, smelly, bitter substance called resin. It deters animals from eating them, traps attacking insects, and seals wounds in the wood.

Oak woods

Oaks have spreading branches with clumps of leaves, letting in plenty of light. This allows many plants and even other trees to flourish beneath them.

Home to hundreds

Oak trees, especially English oaks, provide food and shelter to hundreds of different living things, from squirrels and birds, to butterflies, wasps, mosses and fungi. Ancient oak woods contain the greatest mix of plants and animals.

Great spotted woodpecker

Wood anemone

Bluebell

Badger

Wood sorrel

Yellow archangel

All these living things may dwell in an oak wood. See how many kinds you can spot here.

Bramble

Timberman beetle

Insect wars

For many insects, oak leaves combine a source of food and a place to lay eggs. The trees fight back, filling their leaves with a chemical that's hard to digest. Oaks can make up for lost leaves with a new set in late summer, called their Lammas growth.

Purple hairstreak butterfly caterpillars look like oak buds.

These disguised caterpillars can feed on oak trees without being spotted by hungry birds.

Gall wasp

Spangle galls

Great oak beauty moth caterpillars look like oak twigs.

Kidney galls

Cherry galls

Green tortrix moth caterpillars munch their way through hundreds of oak leaves in early spring.

Oak apple galls

To defend itself, an oak grows hard swellings, called galls, around insect eggs. These house the growing grubs, and provide food when they hatch.

Acorns for all

In autumn, oak twigs are laden with shiny acorns. As well as containing the seeds of new trees, their nutty goodness helps sustain many animals through the winter.

English oak acorns grow on long stalks.

Sessile oak acorns have no stalks, sitting directly on the twig.

A jay may bury as many as 5,000 acorns as a winter supply. Some will grow into new oak trees.

Beech woods

Beech branches form a thick, leafy canopy which stops most of the light from reaching the woodland floor. Few plants are able to grow beneath them.

Life in the shade

Only a handful of trees, such as holly and yew, can thrive alongside beeches. They are evergreen, so they can make food from sunlight all year, and they grow very slowly, so they don't need as much energy as other plants.

Holly can survive in beech's heavy shade.

Brief blooms

Of the flowers that do grow in beech woods, many only last for the short, sunny spell between winter and spring. Others have found ways to endure the gloom.

Cuckoo pint has large leaves to gather as much light as possible.

Solomon's seal grows as tall as it can.

Common dog violet's dark green leaves have extra chlorophyll to make the most of dim light.

The early spring sunlight magically transforms this beech wood floor into a sea of bluebells.

Leafy carpet

Dead beech leaves are tough and take a long time to rot, so beech woods are usually carpeted in leaf litter. This makes it hard for most flowers to grow, but creepy-crawlies flourish.

Snails hide among the damp leaves by day, and feed on them by night.

Wood crickets prowl around, hunting smaller insects in the litter.

Bird's nest orchids don't need sunlight to grow, but live on dead leaves.

Beechnuts

In autumn, beechnuts ripen. Their prickly cases start to split, and the nuts tumble to the woodland floor, where many are gratefully gobbled up by hungry wildlife.

Beechnuts are three-sided and are protected by bristly husks.

A nuthatch makes beechnuts "hatch" out by jamming them into bark and hammering them with its beak.

Wet woods

Most trees can't survive in waterlogged soil,
but a few, such as willow and alder, thrive in
marshy areas, or alongside rivers and streams.

Watery willows

Boggy woodland covered with
willows and alders is known as
carr. It is full of water-loving
plants, and lush undergrowth
where animals and birds
can scurry in safety.

Goat willow

Alder

Great
reedmace

Common
reed

Brooklime

You can find
these plants
in wet woods.

Alders have
small, cone-
like fruits.

Common nettle

Meadowsweet

Sailing seeds

Alders, poplars and willows near water
drop oily-coated seeds onto its surface.
These float away, washing up on other
banks, and may sprout into new trees.

Alder seeds

Ferns

Ferns have been around since prehistoric times. Their large, leafy fronds come in many shapes, from feathery bracken to glossy, crinkled hart's-tongue. Underneath the fronds, you may see tiny, brown clumps of seed-like spores.

Bracken

Ferns grow abundantly in damp places.

Every species has a different pattern of spores.

Spores on bracken

Hard fern

Hart's-tongue fern

Leaf beetle

Redpolls feed on seeds in spring.

Otters and others

Unsurprisingly, wet woods are home to many animals, from frisky otters that fish in the water, to birds such as redpolls, that feast on alder seeds. You'll also find countless insects.

Dragonflies rest on willow leaves in summer.

An otter snoozes on a willow branch hanging over a lazy river.

Cranefly

Town trees

Even if you live in a built-up area, you probably won't have to go far to see trees. They are planted in towns and cities to provide pleasant scenery, but do a whole lot more.

Trees of peace

Trees can help people to relax, and take pride in the places where they live and work. Research has shown that hospital patients recover more quickly when they can see trees, and police report fewer crimes in leafy areas.

Trees attract songbirds and help to muffle traffic noise.

Starling

Plant wisely

If trees are chosen carefully, they can bring many benefits to towns, but trees planted in the wrong places can cause problems.

Rowans have pretty, red berries in summer, but these can make pavements slippery.

In summer, common lime trees give shelter, but also drip with honeydew, a sticky goo made by the aphids that live on them.

London planes grow very well in cities, but their roots can cause pavements to buckle.

Beech offers deep shade, but blocks out light where it's too close to houses.

Air fresheners

As well as producing the oxygen gas that people and animals breathe, some trees actually soak up the poisonous gases that pollute the air of towns and cities.

The bark of London plane withstands air pollution, flaking off regularly to rid itself of harmful chemicals.

Field maple

These trees help to clean up city pollution.

Silver birch

Street survivors

City life can be hard on trees: their branches are often bashed by buses and their roots squashed beneath pavements. They also have to put up with car fumes, vandalism and frequent pruning. Some trees survive cities better than others.

Ginkgoes are unique Asian trees. They are insect-proof and can resist fire, pollution and even nuclear disasters.

Flowering cherry trees like these, planted for their candy-pink blossom, are unlikely to live their full life spans in the parched, paved city streets.

Wood is good

Even in the 21st century, no one has invented a better building material than wood. It is strong, tough and light – and it's very easy to grow.

From log to plank

Trunks and big branches felled for wood are called timber. The logs are taken by truck or boat to sawmills. Each one is sawn in a way that makes as many useful planks as possible.

These will be the widest planks.

Heartwood is strong, and used as building timber.

Leftover wood chips are pulped to make paper. Bark chippings are used in gardening and as animal bedding.

Along the grain

Across the grain

Grain

Every plank has a pattern of lines and whorls, called its grain, made by the yearly growth rings inside the tree. Wood is at its strongest when it is cut along the grain. Cut across the grain, it's more likely to crack and break.

Knots

Base of a branch

Some planks have dark spots, called knots, where the base of a branch was buried in the tree trunk. Knots can weaken wood, but they may also make it look more attractive.

This trunk has been cut lengthways.

Uses of wood

Conifers grow quickly, and their wood, known as softwood, is plentiful. It is used where large quantities of timber are needed, such as for building and paper making. Broadleaved trees grow at a much gentler pace, producing tough, resilient "hardwood". This is often used in making furniture, flooring and musical instruments.

The colour, strength and suppleness of these trees makes their wood useful for different purposes.

Cherry wood is used to make fine furniture.

Solid and sturdy, oak is ideal for beams and floors.

Spruce carries sound well and is used in instrument making.

This violin was crafted from a number of woods, each one selected for its qualities.

Processed wood

A lot of the wood you see has been processed to strengthen it, or to produce items more quickly and cheaply than it's possible to do using natural wood.

Grain

Plywood is thin layers of wood glued together to make it stronger.

Veneer

Cutting blade

Veneer is a thin sheet of wood with a decorative grain, glued onto cheap, plain wood.

Forest harvest

People have always harvested trees for their wood, but they provide much more besides.

Fruit 'n' nut

It's not just animals that eat fruit and nuts. People relish their sweet flavours, and need the vital vitamins and nourishment they give.

Walnuts can help keep your heart healthy.

Walnuts grow in leathery, green jackets.

Sweet chestnuts are often roasted before eating.

These succulent plums are brimful of vitamins which can help your body fight disease.

Healing trees

Lots of trees contain chemicals that scientists have developed into medicines. Aspirin, used to soothe headaches and fevers, is based on a chemical found in willow bark.

Oil from eucalyptus leaves is used in cough and cold remedies.

A chemical in yew bark is used to fight cancer.

Herbs and spices

Cinnamon bark

Juniper berries

Bay leaves

Many parts of trees are used in cooking. The leaves of bay laurel add a savoury tang to soups and stews. The bark of cinnamon trees is ground into a fragrant spice, and juniper trees have berry-like fruits which are dried and used to season strongly flavoured meats.

Silkworms

The leaves of white mulberry trees provide a home and food for silk moth caterpillars. These spin cocoons with a soft, strong thread, which can be woven into the finest, shimmering silks.

Silkworm

White mulberry leaves

A single silkworm cocoon can contain up to 900m (3,000ft) of unbroken silk thread.

Silkworms turn into silk moths.

Snuffle a truffle

Although many woodland fungi are poisonous, a few are edible. Some, such as porcini and chanterelle, are fairly common. Truffles are rare, potato-shaped fungi that grow under tree roots. They are highly prized because they're difficult to find.

Chanterelle mushrooms often grow by beech trees.

Porcini mushrooms are also known as ceps or penny buns.

Black truffle

In Italy and France, pigs are trained to sniff out truffles.

Working with trees

People have worked with trees for centuries, planting and pruning them to grow in useful ways. Most woods have been carefully managed for at least part of their lifetime.

Traditional trimming

Coppicing is an ancient way of managing trees by cutting them down to a stump, or "stool". Multiple shoots then grow into straight sticks which have many uses, from basket-making to building.

The shoots of a coppiced stump grow long and straight.

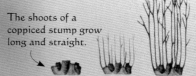

In another old method, pollarding, the tops of trees are cut off some way above the ground so grazing animals can't eat their shoots. Trees in towns are often pollarded so they don't overshadow houses, or tangle in overhead wires.

A farmer has pollarded this row of willow trees to produce a harvest of useful sticks, called wands or withies.

Forestry today

Forestry is about farming trees for timber, both in wild woods and in man-made ones, called plantations. Foresters use various methods to ensure new crops of trees will grow.

Mechanical tree harvesters, like this, have a rotating arm to grip large trunks, and a circular saw to cut them up.

In clearcutting, a small patch of trees is felled. Those left produce seeds for new trees.

The seed tree system takes trees from a wide area, leaving a few behind for reseeding.

In selective felling, the strongest trees are left to grow longest, to produce wood of the best quality.

Planting out

To prepare a new plantation, ground must first be cleared and ploughed. Young trees are planted about 4m apart: that's about 63,000 trees in a square kilometre.

Seedlings are planted out when they are about 20 times as tall as this picture.

Changing times

Plantations of conifers grow more quickly than broadleaf ones, making for more regular harvests, but few animals can live in them. Conifer plantations were once most common but today, foresters plant more broadleaves, and care for wildlife.

Plantation of conifers

Protecting trees

Sustainable forestry is a way of working that carefully controls the pace at which trees are felled and replanted, to keep forests and their wildlife healthy for the future.

Vanishing forests

Forests, especially tropical rainforests, are not always looked after in a sustainable way. Around the world, every minute, an area of trees the size of 37 football pitches is lost as forests are cleared for farmland, or harvested to make timber or fuel.

In some places, only certain trees are selected for logging. This allows the forest to regrow at its own pace.

"Slash and burn" is a way of creating farmland by felling and burning trees. Crops grow for a short time, but soon the dusty soil is useless, so more land is needed and more trees must be sacrificed.

Chopping down trees is an easy way to make money, even where it is illegal.

No place like home

Tropical rainforests are huge, evergreen, broadleaf forests in hot, wet parts of South America, Africa and Asia. They are home to the world's greatest variety of life, but are being wiped out faster than any other forests. Amazing animals and valuable plants are in danger of dying out.

The forest home of these orang-utans in Borneo is being destroyed so quickly, to make oil palm plantations, that they may die out in the next five years.

Poison arrow frogs are made homeless as the rainforest vanishes.

Rosy periwinkles are rare rainforest flowers, used to make cancer medicine.

What can you do?

You can help save the world's trees by being careful how you use tree products:

- Use both sides of a piece of paper.
- Use recycled paper: it's made from used paper so it doesn't harm any more trees.
- Recycle as much paper as you can yourself.
- Check that paper and wood products you use are labelled "sustainable", or have a mark proving they came from well-managed forests.

This mark shows paper is made from wood from well-managed forests.

This symbol means that a product can be recycled.

Trees of the world

Around the globe, trees grow in surprising ways as they adapt to life in extremely varied conditions.

North America

The USA is home to some very tough trees. Joshua trees are spike-leaved evergreens that survive in the parched Mojave desert. In Florida, mangrove trees flourish in the salty, coastal swamps.

Mangroves prop themselves up above the briny water on stilt-like roots, as you can see in this photo.

South America

The rainforests of Brazil contain a vast array of plant life, including towering giants, such as red meranti, and cacao trees, from which chocolate is made.

Cacao tree flowers grow on the trunk, and turn into pod-like fruit.

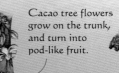

The pods hold seeds that are used to make chocolate.

Some very tall rainforest trees have shallow roots. Their trunks flare out at the base for extra support.

Europe

Tamarisks grow in salty, seaside areas in many parts of Europe. In the Canary Islands, near Morocco, umbrella-shaped dragon trees are found.

Dragon trees take their name from their sticky red resin, known as dragon's blood, which is used as a dye.

Tamarisk

In summer, tamarisks are covered in clusters of tiny pink flowers.

Asia

A banyan, or "strangler fig", starts life on the branches of another tree. Its roots snake groundwards around the trunk, until they eventually smother their host to death, and the banyan takes its place.

Banyans are some of the world's widest trees.

Africa

African acacias have a parasol shape because all their lower leaves are eaten by giraffes. Baobabs are tubby trees that look like they're upside-down with their roots in the air.

Baobabs can store enough water in their trunks to last for nine months without rain.

On many African plains, acacias are all that grow.

Tree tales

There's something mysterious about trees. They've inspired countless myths and magical stories, and are important symbols in many religions.

Robin Hood

The legends of the cunning outlaw Robin Hood centre on Sherwood Forest in England. He and his companions, the Merry Men, are said to have hidden in its green depths from the wicked Sheriff of Nottingham. A tree called the Major Oak, alive today, is said to have been their hideout.

Robin Hood is said to have dressed in green to hide among the trees of Sherwood Forest.

Tears and flowers

In one Greek myth, a princess, Phyllis, loved a soldier named Acamas. He went off to war for ten years, and she nearly died of heartbreak. A kind goddess saved Phyllis by turning her into an almond tree. On his return, Acamas sadly kissed the leafless tree. All at once, it burst into flower.

Almond trees blossom before their leaves appear. The story of Phyllis tells why.

A German legend

One Christmas night, Martin Luther, a churchman, was walking home through the woods. Inspired by the starlight twinkling in the trees, he took a little fir tree home to his family, and set candles in its branches to represent the stars.

The two trees

The Bible tells the story of the Garden of Eden. God told Adam and Eve, the first people, that they might eat the fruit of any tree except the Tree of the Knowledge of Good and Evil. They disobeyed God, and were banished from Eden, so they could not eat from the Tree of Life, which would have let them live forever.

A sly serpent misled Eve by twisting God's words, and she ate the fruit of the forbidden tree.

The world tree

The Vikings believed that the universe was held together by the roots of a giant ash tree, named Yggdrasil. One root passed through Asgard, the dwelling-place of gods and elves. Another ran through Midgard, the human world, and the last plunged into Niflheim, the frozen land of the dead.

Yggdrasil, the cosmic ash

Amazing but true

Time traveller
Ginkgoes are Chinese trees that lived before the dinosaurs. Fossils show that prehistoric ginkgoes were very similar to those alive today.

Ginkgo

Fossilized leaf of an early ginkgo

Mexican marvel
In Oaxaca, Mexico, is the world's fattest tree. Known as the Tule Tree, this Montezuma cypress is 35.8m (117½ft) around. It takes 26 men holding hands to encircle its trunk.

Medicine trees
A quarter of all medicines contain chemicals found in trees and plants from the steamy rainforests of South America and Asia.

Many rainforest plants have healing power.

Reach for the sky
The world's tallest tree is a coast redwood in California, USA. Named Hyperion, it is 115.2m (378ft) high – taller than London's Big Ben.

Coast redwood

General giant
General Sherman, a giant sequoia, is the bulkiest living thing on Earth. Growing in Sequoia National Park, California, it measures 83.8m (275ft) high by 31.3m (102½ft) around the base.

Supersize cone
The longest cones come from sugar pines, which grow in the USA. They can measure 66cm (26in) – that's over two-thirds the length of a cricket bat.

Sugar pine cone

Mammoth fruit

The jackfruit tree of India has the largest fruit of any broadleaf or conifer. The prickly, yellow-green fruit can be up to 90cm (35in) long and 50cm (20in) wide, and weigh 34kg (75lb) – as much as a ten-year-old boy.

These ripening jackfruit smell like rotting onions, but taste more like pineapple.

Protection points

African acacias guard their leaves with thorns, but giraffes still reach them with their long, flexible tongues. So, as soon as the nibbling begins, the trees produce a foul-tasting chemical. The giraffes soon leave to find a tastier tree.

Thorns

Bristlecone pine

Old as the hills

Bristlecone pines in the dry, harsh surroundings of the Californian White Mountains can only survive by growing very slowly. One pine, nicknamed Methuselah, is over 4,770 years old. It was a seedling when the pyramids of Egypt were being built.

Digging deep

One wild fig tree in South Africa was found to have roots tunnelling down to 120m (400ft) underground.

Far-flung forest

Earth's largest stretch of unbroken forest is the East Siberian taiga. With an area of 3,900,000km^2 (1,500,000 square miles), it covers over a fifth of Russia.

Ant apartment

A bullhorn acacia has a special relationship with ants. It lets an army of the insects live inside its huge thorns, and even makes tiny food parcels for them. In return, the ants sting animals that try to eat the tree.

This ant has collected a food parcel from its host's leaf-tips.

Food parcels

INDEX

age 30–31, 63
animals 7, 23, 30, 33, 35, 37, 41, 42, 43, 47, 57
bark 15, 37, 40, 49, 50, 52
birds 7, 23, 25, 33, 35, 41, 42, 43, 45, 47, 48
branches 13, 18, 31, 50
broadleaf trees 9, 51
buds 16–17, 29
catkins 21, 37
chlorophyll 10, 26, 44
climate 19, 58–59
cones 8, 25, 28, 37, 62
conifers 8, 11, 28, 40–41, 51
deciduous trees 9
evergreen trees 8, 28, 44
ferns 30, 39, 47

flowers 20–21, 22, 34, 40, 42, 44, 45, 46, 57, 60
forestry 55, 56, 57
fruits 9, 22–24, 39, 52, 63
fungi 7, 30, 32, 34, 38, 40, 53
galls 43
grain 50, 51
heartwood 14, 31, 50
insects 7, 21, 23, 32, 33, 35, 36, 41, 42, 43, 47, 48, 63
leaves 8, 9, 10–11, 12, 16, 17, 26–27, 28, 35, 37, 40, 43, 45, 53
lichen 30, 39
life span 7, 30, 49, 63
moss 39
nuts 23, 37, 45, 52

paper 50, 57
parasites 32, 38–39
pollen 20, 21
rainforests 57, 58, 62
recycling 57
resin 41, 59
roots 12, 17, 48, 58
sap 12, 14–15
sapwood 14
seedlings 16–17, 55
seeds 8, 16, 20, 22–25, 43, 46, 55
shrubs 6
tree rings 14
trunks 6, 9, 12, 13, 14–15, 30–31, 55, 58, 59, 62
wood 33, 34, 50–51, 57

ACKNOWLEDGEMENTS

Cover design: Joanne Kirkby
Additional designs: Nayera Everall and Reuben Barrance
Artwork co-ordinator: Louise Breen
With thanks to Mike Olley

PHOTO CREDITS (t = top, m = middle, b = bottom, l = left, r = right)
1 © Martin Ruegner/Stone/Getty Images; 2–3 © Tohoku Color Agency/Japan Images/Getty Images; 4–5 © David Boag/Alamy; 6b © Phil Seale/Alamy; 8bl © Ellen McKnight/Alamy; 10b © blickwinkel/Alamy; 13 © dbphots/Alamy; 15r © Keith Levit/Alamy; 16bl © The Garden Picture Library/Alamy; 19b © Ken Welsh/Alamy; 20l © GAP Photos/Mark Bolton; 23b © Martin Ruegner/Stone/Getty Images; 24m © Michael P. Gadomski/Science Photo Library; 26b © Nicholas Frost/Alamy; 28b © Peter Arnold, Inc/Alamy; 31 © Archie Miles/Alamy; 33tr © Dave Watts/Alamy; 35br © Arco Images/Alamy; 36tl © Lars S. Madsen/Alamy; 38bl © Steve Austin, Papilio/CORBIS; 44–45 © Kevin Schafer/CORBIS; 47b © David Hosking/Alamy; 49 © Niels-DK/Alamy; 51bl © bildagentur-online.com/th-foto/Alamy; 51r © Junior Gonzalez/fStop/Getty Images; 52r © ImageDJ/Alamy; 54l © blickwinkel/Alamy; 57t © Digital Vision; 58b © Peter Arnold, Inc/Alamy; 63t © Paul Thompson/CORBIS

ILLUSTRATORS Bob Bampton, John Barber, Joyce Bee, Isabel Bowring, Trevor Boyer, Wendy Bramall, Paul Brooks, Hilary Burn, Kuo Kang Chen, Frankie Coventry, Christina Darter, Peter Dennis, Michelle Emblem, Sandra Fernandez, Denise Finney, Sarah Fox-Davies, John Francis, Keith Furnival, Sheila Galbraith, William Giles, Victoria Goaman, Victoria Gordon, Tim Hayward, Christine Howes, David Hurrell, Ian Jackson, Steven Kirk, Jonathan Langley, Mick Loates, Rachel Lockwood, Andy Martin, Malcolm McGregor, Dee McLean, Annabel Milne, David More, Robert Morton, Tricia Newell, Barbara Nicholson, David Palmer, Julie Piper, Barrie Raynor, Michelle Ross, Chris Shields, Peter Stebbing, Ralph Stobart, Elena Temporin, Ron Tiner, Sally Voke, Phil Weare, Gerald Wood, James Woods, David Wright and others